As Kris came to the top of the hill he came to a sudden stop. What he saw was beyond wonderful.

He knew instantly that it was a Rocket Car. Not just a run-of-the-mill Rocket Car, but a shiny, red, mega-turbo, all-terrain Rocket Car. The bubble over the cockpit suddenly raised, and Kris climbed inside before you could snap your fingers. In no time, he was wearing a silver racing helmet and a pair of driving gloves, and the Rocket Car roared to a start. . . .

HOOMANIA

A JOURNEY INTO PROVERBS

Michael P. Waite

Chariot Books
David C. Cook Publishing Co.

Chariot Books is an imprint of David C. Cook Publishing Co.
David C. Cook Publishing Co., Elgin, Illinois 60120
David C. Cook Publishing Co., Weston, Ontario

HOOMANIA—A JOURNEY INTO PROVERBS
© 1987 by Michael P. Waite for text and inside illustrations.
© 1985 Hoomania Partners, Ltd., for cover photograph.
Cover photograph by Rick Garside

Cover design by Warren Kramer

First printing, 1987
Printed in the United States of America
92 91 90 89 88 87   5 4 3 2 1

Library of Congress Cataloging-in-Publication Data
Waite, Michael P.
  Hoomania—a journey into proverbs
  Summary: An encounter with an inventor and a game he has created zaps Kris into a fantastic world of crazy characters, where his race to Mount Wizzdom brings him knowledge about responsible choices to please his parents and God.
  [1. Conduct of life—Fiction. 2. Christian life—Fiction. 3. Fantasy.]
I. Title.
PZ7.W1333Ho 1987   [Fic]   87-21279
ISBN 1-55513-637-0

Acknowledgments

I first wrote *Hoomania* as a screenplay which was later produced as an animated film by Rick Garside and myself. Although I've changed the story quite a bit in writing this book, I'm sure many of the touches given by my film companions remain intact. For this reason, I wish to thank everyone who worked on the film, *Hoomania*, and I especially want to acknowledge certain artists from whom I have "borrowed" the most.

Many of the character illustrations in this book are based on characters designed for animation by Jill and Gary Trousdale and Tony and Barbara DeRosa. I dedicate this book to them hoping they'll forgive me for turning their designs into such pitiful scribblings. Also, they have illustrated several of my books (published by David C. Cook) and I owe them immeasurable gratitude (though they'd much rather get a decent check).

Credit is also due to Rick Garside who directed the film version of *Hoomania* and has inevitably contributed in various ways to the story as it now stands. Finally, I must thank Alice Robie, who was the Executive Producer of the film version. Without her there would be no film, and probably no book.

MPW

Contents

1
A Window Gets in the Way

Kris Atwood had never been so bored in all his life. His big sister, who Kris called "the Muskrat," was away at summer camp. So he had no one to pick on. Right after she had left, Kris was caught turning the clothes hamper into a spider farm. So his parents grounded him.

No more going to the lake to swim. No more going on Walter Peaver's bike jump. And no more leaving the yard for five whole days! What a boring way to spend the summer.

And if being bored wasn't bad enough, while Kris was sitting out in his yard, Davey Bortel came over and wanted to trade baseball cards. Kris couldn't stand Davey Bortel. Davey was the kind of kid who put stickers all over things. He whined when he

talked. He ate black licorice. And he cried whenever he fell. Davey didn't like Kris either, but he needed someone to bother.

"You don't have any good cards," Davey said, making sure to bend each of Kris's cards as he sorted through them.

"They're as good as yours!" Kris huffed.

Davey ignored Kris and looked around for something to do. He saw Kris's baseball and bat sitting on the lawn.

"Hey, wanna toss the ball around?" Davey said.

"Naw," Kris answered, wishing Davey would go away.

"I'll make a bet with you!" Davey coaxed.

"What kind of bet?" Kris said, rolling over on the

grass.

"I'll bet you ten baseball cards that you can't hit the ball over the roof of your house!" Davey said with a disgusting smile. He had black licorice all over his teeth.

"Oh, sure, Davey!" Kris snapped. "And what if I break a window?"

"You're chicken!" Davey gloated.

"I'm not chicken, I just don't—" Kris started to say.

"You're chicken!" Davey shouted. "Chicken-chicken-chicken!" And with that he began dancing around the lawn squawking like a chicken gone haywire.

"All right! All right!" Kris cried. "It's a bet. Ten baseball cards . . . and I get to pick the ones I want!"

"Sure," Davey said, glowing with that sickening smile. "And if you lose, I get to pick ten of yours!"

"Huh!" Kris scoffed. He picked up the ball and bat and stood in front of the house looking for the best place to hit. The roof over the garage looked good. It didn't look all that high, and the nearest window was way over in the living room. It would be a cinch!

Even so, a little Voice between his ears started raising a commotion. "Don't be a fool!" the Voice argued. "You aren't even supposed to play catch in front of the house. Just think what's gonna happen if you hit a ball through that big picture window!"

Kris had completely forgotten about his mother's

Number One Regulation for playing outdoors: No baseball in the front yard. The Voice had brought up a good point. Maybe this bet wasn't such a great idea.

"What's takin' so long?" Davey sneered. "You aren't gonna chicken out are you?" And he smiled with rotten delight, exposing all of those gooey, black teeth.

Kris suddenly forgot about the second thoughts. He wasn't going to take all this garbage from a little weasel like Davey. He braced himself for the hit, holding the ball in his left hand.

"Ignore that little stinker!" the Voice persisted. "He doesn't care if you get in trouble. Tell him to get lost. Who cares if he calls you a chicken?"

Kris paused again. Davey could see the doubt on his face.

"I knew it!" Davey roared. "You're a chicken! A chicken and a loser! Hand over those baseball cards and—"

But Kris didn't give him time to finish. He threw the ball up in the air and swung the bat with everything he had, aiming above the garage roof.

The ball went fast and hard, and if it had gone in the right direction it would have been a very good hit. But instead, it shot off to the right and blasted straight through the big picture window with an enormous CRASH! It sounded like a bomb exploding. Glass flew everywhere. Even pieces of the windowpane were smashed out. Kris stood in sick disbelief for a long while, staring as little pieces of glass tinkled and tumbled onto the living room floor. Davey wasn't quite so surprised by the disaster though, and he quickly disappeared down the street.

"Kristopher Atwood!" came an angry voice from inside the house. Kris suddenly realized his predicament and jumped into the hedge beside the house.

Footsteps rushed into the living room, and Kris could hear his parents' gasps of horror coming through the window above him. Then, there was a long, terrible pause of silence, and finally, he heard his father say something like, "Don't you worry, I'll get through to that son of ours this time!" And something about "the seat of his pants."

There was much, much more, but Kris didn't stick around to hear it. He figured he was dead, and it was time to disappear. He made a run for the bushes beside the Hertsons' house and dove into them without being spotted.

His best bet, he decided, was to run away. Maybe he could join a circus or a rock band or something. But one thing was for sure, he didn't want to face his mom and dad! Not after this one.

He scrambled through the bushes and yanked his bike out of its hiding place. He took a shortcut across the Hertsons' lawn, through the Bortels' back gate, around most of Mrs. Kimble's flower garden, and peddled down the street to start a life of exile.

2
Sam Weatherfield's Workshop

Kris really couldn't think of many places to hide out. He sort of wanted to jump onto a train and sneak out of town in a boxcar. But he wasn't allowed to ride his bike near the railroad tracks. He also thought it would be neat to hide in a banana crate on a ship headed for Africa. But there weren't any ships in town. There weren't any oceans either. So Kris had to come up with an easier plan. He went to Sam Weatherfield's workshop.

Mr. Weatherfield was an inventor. He didn't invent regular things like can openers and garden tools. He made strange, wonderful things like rocket-powered skateboards and mechanical dinosaurs.

Kris went to visit Mr. Weatherfield quite often. They had become good friends and Kris got to try

14

out a lot of Sam's inventions. Kris also went to Mr. Weatherfield's workshop every time he ran away—which was not an uncommon event.

Kris parked his bike behind an old truck in Mr. Weatherfield's driveway. He stuck his head inside the workshop door and called inside. "Mr. Weatherfield? Mr. Weatherfield . . . are you in here?"

The only response was the buzzing and whirring of motors, the gurgling and bubbling of experiments, and the creaking and squeaking of machines. So Kris stepped into the shop.

As usual, the place was a mess. There were old radios and broken televisions and electric motors and wheels and pipes and wires. Mr. Weatherfield had "organized" them into tall, jumbled piles that climbed from the floor to the ceiling. (And he quite frankly thought it was a very practical system.)

In between the piles, there were maps and charts nailed to the walls. They looked like scribble drawings all covered with numbers, and Kris never paid much attention to them because they reminded him of math. In the center of the room, there were a few inventions that Kris hadn't seen before. One looked like a lawn mower with wings. Also, there was a big plastic castle full of white mice. They were all wearing little suits, and some of them were riding around in tiny race cars. Kris was going to stop and play with them for a while, but he spotted Mr. Weatherfield in the back of the shop.

Mr. Weatherfield was sitting in front of a funny-looking machine, holding three stalks of corn, and wearing a pair of headphones. He was concentrating so hard that his face was all wrinkled up like a raisin. He suddenly noticed Kris and smiled, signaling for Kris to come closer. The funny-looking machine was making an awful noise, and sparks were hissing and flickering between the wires. Kris walked up to Mr. Weatherfield, trying to keep some distance from the machine.

"What's this thing?" Kris shouted, trying to talk above the noise.

"I call it the 'Model V-800 Veggie Verbalizer,'" Sam said proudly.

"What does it do?" said Kris just as a flash of sparks went off.

"It uses a tiny microphone to pick up sounds coming from inside plants," Mr. Weatherfield explained.

"What for?" said Kris.

"Well . . . then we can amplify those sounds and record them, and find out what sort of noises a plant makes. See?" Mr. Weatherfield smiled brightly.

"Oh, I get it," Kris said. "You want to see what plants talk about, huh?"

But Mr. Weatherfield didn't have time to answer his question. Suddenly, a shower of sparks shot out of the machine and the cornstalks burst into fire. A horrible shriek blared out of Mr. Weatherfield's headphones, knocking them right off his head. And

finally, the whole contraption went up in a blaze of sparks and smoke and flames. All that was left on the table was a little black bundle of wire and some badly burnt popcorn.

Slowly, the smoke cleared away.

"I guess it still needs a little work," Sam chuckled, taking a rag from his pocket. "So, Kristopher, what brings you over to visit me?"

"Aw, nothin' much," said Kris. "I'm just runnin' away, that's all."

"Oh . . . well . . . if that's all," said Mr. Weatherfield, cleaning off the table with a rag.

"I busted the front window with a baseball," Kris added without much concern. "But it wasn't my fault! That jerky kid, Davey Bortel, bet me I couldn't hit it over the roof."

"Looks like he won the bet," said Mr. Weatherfield. "I suppose that's who you're running away from?"

"No way! I'm not afraid of Davey Bortel. He couldn't hurt a flea!" Kris replied. "I had to run away 'cause of my parents. They're gonna ground me 'til I'm fifty years old. And they'll probably spank me so hard I could never sit down again!"

"Well, then," said Mr. Weatherfield. "I expect you'll be running up to Canada or Mexico or someplace safe?"

"No, I was thinking I'd just hide out here," Kris said, picking through the burnt pieces of cornstalk.

"What? You don't mean here in my workshop?"

Sam jumped up dramatically. "I'd be arrested for housing an escaped convict! They'd send me to jail and—"

"Aw, come on, Mr. Weatherfield, don't tease!" Kris said crossly. "I'm dead if I go home."

Mr. Weatherfield smiled and put his hand on Kris's shoulder. "Now, how many times does this make?"

"What do you mean?" Kris pretended to be innocent. "I haven't got in trouble that much."

"No?" Sam laughed. "How about the time you went snake hunting with Billy Brickly—remember that? Afterwards, you put a whole jar of grass snakes in that girl's desk at school?"

"That was Billy's idea!" Kris argued.

"And the time you cut down the tree that Stanley Norton had built his tree house in?" Sam continued.

"Yeah, but he deserved it!" Kris said, beginning to feel angry. "So, what's the big deal anyway? Everybody acts as if I'm some kind of criminal or something. I don't get in trouble on purpose. . . . It just happens. If other kids weren't always buggin' me I'd probably never get in trouble."

Mr. Weatherfield couldn't think of anything more to say. He could see that Kris wasn't much in the mood for listening. So he finished cleaning up his mess while he searched his inventor's brain for some clever answer to Kris's problem.

And then, a very bright idea hit him. Without another word, he went to a cabinet on the other side of the workshop and took an old wooden box down from the shelf. He brushed some junk off from a worktable and set the box down.

Kris was glad to have the subject of his behavior over with, and was hoping that Sam was getting out some kind of wonderful new invention. He crossed the room to see what the inventor was doing.

It was a long, flat box with some faded letters on the top. It read:

HOOMANIA

"What's that mean?" said Kris.

"It's a game I invented," said Mr. Weatherfield, and he opened the box. He took out a colorful game board with all sorts of strange cartoon people drawn onto it. There was also a glass mountain that went together in pieces, a spinner, some cards, a timer, and a whole bunch of funny-looking game tokens.

"Wow!" gasped Kris. "Wanna play?"

"I can't right now," said Sam. "But you can play this game by yourself. It's really quite easy . . . if you're careful and you use your head."

"I'm pretty good at that kind of stuff," Kris said, anxious to get started.

"All you need to do," Sam instructed, "is stay on this colored trail. . . . See the little signs? Wherever it says 'Path to Mount Wizzdom,' that's where you want to go."

"Mount Wizzdom?" said Kris, thinking he'd heard that word before.

"Right," Sam continued. "When you get inside the Gates of Wizzdom at the top of the Mountain, that means you've won the game."

"Easy!" Kris said, and grabbed a game token.

"Now, wait a minute," Sam continued. "You've gotta watch out for tricks! There's a lot of traps waiting for you—things to get you off the Path. And if you make a wrong move, you get one of these." Sam held up one of the cards. It had a goofy, blue bird with crossed eyes on one side, and on the other side it said:

Dodo Bird

"This is a Dodo Bird Card," the inventor grinned. "If you get three of these, you lose."

"I won't lose!" Kris boasted trying to place his game piece on the board. Sam caught his hand.

"One more thing," Sam added. "You only have thirty minutes to finish the game!" Sam set the timer for thirty minutes. A starting bell went off—it was almost as loud as a fire alarm.

"That's an awful short time for a game," Kris complained.

"It's plenty of time for someone who's careful and wise!" Sam started to walk away from the table. "Just let me know when you're finished. I want to know how you do. Good luck!"

"Okay," Kris said with a self-assured smile. "I'll probably finish early, 'cause I usually win at games."

Mr. Weatherfield stepped out into his back room

leaving Kris with the game. It was so sparkly and colorful that Kris couldn't wait to get started. Besides, the timer was running, so he figured he'd better hurry. He made himself comfortable in a big, puffy chair and picked up his game piece to start the game. He set it down on a colored circle that said "Start," and a tingling feeling came shooting up through his arms and into his whole body. He was feeling very strange all of a sudden, and he noticed that his whole body was surrounded by a bright blue light. He tried to shout for Mr. Weatherfield, but he was much too late. The blue light sucked him up like a vacuum cleaner, and Kristopher Atwood disappeared into the game called *HOOMANIA*.

3

The Journey Begins

Kris fell through the air helplessly. The blue light was swirling around him, and he could feel himself shrinking at a tremendous speed. By the time he hit the ground—which he did with a painful "Oomph!" —he wasn't much larger than a beetle. Worse still, he had landed in a very strange place. Mr. Weatherfield's workshop was nowhere in sight.

Kris stood up rubbing his bottom and looking around curiously. He had never seen anything like this place before. The hills were shaped like candy drops, and they came in all sorts of different colors. There were odd little trees that shined and sparkled as they grew along the hillsides. And there was a beautiful pathway made of enormous, flat rocks that were painted all sorts of bright colors.

"Where in the world am I?" Kris asked himself aloud.

"Hoomania!" squealed a voice behind him. And several other voices giggled loudly.

Kris spun around, quite startled, and found himself eye-to-eye with three enormous Game Tokens (much like the ones you place on a game board, except they had big eyes and ridiculous smiles). One was red, one was green, and one was blue. They were wheezing with laughter and staring at him foolishly.

"You're in Hoomania!" the Red Token repeated, and resumed snickering.

Kris just stared. He'd never seen anything plastic talk before.

"Aren't you gonna play?!" said the Yellow Token. His friends chimed in with a round of giggles.

"Well . . . uh . . . what do I do?" said Kris, still a little shaken.

"Turn the spinwheel!" they all shouted together. "Turn the spinwheel!" And they followed this with a chorus of blubbering laughter.

Indeed, there was a gigantic spinwheel beside the pathway. It was painted in different-colored pie shapes, and there was a big, black arrow balanced in the center. Kris gave the spinner a gentle shove. Nothing happened.

"Harder!" squealed the Tokens. "Spin it harder!" And they giggled uncontrollably.

Kris wound up and gave the spinner a good, solid

push, and it spun around so fast that it hurled him
off into a clump of purple bushes. It spun for a
while, then slowed, and slowed, and stopped. The
ground began to rumble and tremble, and out of the
spinner hopped four little men shaped like arrows.
They were all different colors and had moustaches.
They jumped so high that it looked as if they'd been
shot from a crossbow. Up they went, soaring to the
edge of sight until they looked like tiny little dots,
and then down they fell, landing—one, two, three,
and four. Immediately, the chubby one began
pounding his stomach like a drum, another one
made a deep, groaning noise like a tuba, and all four
of them started marching to the rhythm. Kris
clapped his hands and marched along beside them
with the greatest delight. Their song went like this:

Down the Path to Mount Wizzdom you go!
Hey, there! Hi, there! Whaddaya know!
Don'tchya dare doddle, don'tchya go slow!
Zip-along, skip-along! Off-off you go!

Right on the Path to Mount Wizzdom you stay!
On it! Doggone it! Whaddaya say!
Don'tchya get off it! Don'tchya dare stray!
Romp-along, tromp-along! Have a nice day!

So, you see, the song was actually instructions for
Kris. He usually didn't care much for instructions.
But given in song and dance by people who looked
like arrows, they weren't so bad. So Kris kept right
on marching down the colored path, the Arrows,

26

drumming and humming, stayed behind, and the Tokens giggled foolishly from the hillside.

The Pathway roamed pleasantly over hills and through tunnels and across a couple of streams. It was all so magnificent that Kris wasn't in the least bit concerned about hurrying to finish the game in time. In fact, by now, he'd quite forgotten that he was playing a game at all! Rather, he was feeling very adventurous and perhaps even a bit mischievous, when suddenly, he came to a split in the Path.

There were two large signs at the intersection. One sign pointed straight ahead down the colored Pathway. It was shaped like a pointing finger and on it was written:

The Path to Mount Wizzdom

And off, to the left went a path that was simply labeled,

Shortcut

"Hmmmmm," Kris sighed. "A shortcut. . . . I'll bet it's lots cooler than the regular path. . . ."

Kris remembered quite well that the Arrows had given him instructions not to leave the Path to Mount Wizzdom, and he was having a terrible time deciding which way to go. The Shortcut was a grey path and didn't look quite so pretty as the Path he was on. But it cut back into the hills, and Kris imagined that it probably went all sorts of magical places.

27

"Maybe those little Arrow guys didn't know about this shortcut," Kris told himself. "It's probably a million miles shorter than the colored one. . . . That's why it's called a shortcut!"

Having convinced himself to his liking, Kris started down the Shortcut trail with great curiousity and excitement (and, of course, forgetting Sam's warnings and the Arrows' instructions altogether).

Kris had figured correctly that it would be an interesting path. It had all sorts of odd things growing beside it. There were tall, bushy trees that grew clusters of dice. And when the wind blew, dice would come rolling down their stumps (and they nearly always came up double sixes!). There were bushes that grew tiddledywinks and flowers that looked like blossoming jacks and there was a quarry of dominos carved into a hillside. Then the Shortcut dipped into a little valley and turned into a Tunnel. Kris loved exploring dark, sneaky places, so he stepped right into the hole without giving it a thought.

But the floor of this Tunnel was as slippery as butter, and both of his feet came out from under him, setting Kris onto the seat of his pants. Worse yet, the floor dropped off right where Kris hit the ground, and away he went, sliding downhill into the darkness. It was like an enormous slide—the sort you find in amusement parks. It was slick and greasy, and getting steeper by the second. Kris was scared out of his wits and screaming as down, down he went, rocketing helplessly into the dark. Around nasty curves and over bumps that left his heart up in the air. Poor Kris couldn't tell whether he was upside down or right side up—only that he was flying through darkness at an awful speed. Then, there was one last bump, and Kris flew out of the Tunnel and landed in a fluffy, yellow flower bed.

Kris lay there for a moment waiting for his heart to catch up with him. The Tunnel had brought him into a wonderful, secret valley with lots of little caves and hideaways tucked into the hillsides. And such colors! All around him, the world was glowing like a rainbow.

While Kris sat in the flowers plotting his course through the wonderland, an enormous fellow slid out from behind one of the hills. (The fellow slid because he had no feet—he was a Game Token and he slid about on a large round base.) He was several times bigger than Kris, and his sudden appearance gave the boy quite a start.

Kris was just wondering what he should do when a smaller fellow jumped out from behind the big one; he tipped his hat in a cheery fashion, and slid up to Kris gracefully.

"A jolly, jolly fine day!" said the shorter fellow, reaching to shake Kris's hand. "I'm Derrick, and this here's me pal Erp." He pointed to the big guy. "Jolly fine day for a bit of adventure, wouldn't you say?"

"Yes . . . it is . . ." Kris stuttered.

"I was just sayin' to Erp here, 'Erp me good man, it's a fine day for adventure, and I sure wishes we could find us some good company.' And then I looks around the corner and there you sits. And a strong lookin' lad I should say! Come on, now . . . I'll bet you're tough as a Testy Tiger, aren't you? Strong and fast! There it is! Just what it takes my boy! A lad fittin' for adventure, I'd say. Wouldn't you say, Erp?"

Erp nodded stupidly. "Yup, that's wud I'd say alrighty."

"Well, actually sir, I'm on an adventure right now," Kris announced proudly.

"Jolly good! Cheery then!" Derrick praised him, giving him a hearty slap on the shoulder. "And what sort of an adventure, might I ask? Off to the Diamond Dens, I'll bet! No, no . . . too easy for a burly lad like you. You're goin' after the Dragon's hoard, that's it! Magic and riches, that's the ticket!"

"Nope. Even better!" said Kris, feeling quite pleased that he looked so brave and adventurous. "I'm goin' to the *Gates of Wizzdom!*"

"Gates of Wizzdom?" said Derrick beginning to snicker.

"Gades ub Widzdum?" snorted Erp, starting to chuckle.

And then the both of them burst into laughter. They laughed so hard that they had to hang onto one another to keep from falling down. They slapped their knees, and staggered about, and laughed until

30

tears dribbled down their cheeks. Finally Derrick got ahold of himself enough so that he could talk again.

"That ain't no adventure!" he snorted, still wiping tears from his eyes. "The Gates of Wizzdom is sissy stuff! Why, a tough dapper like you ought to be off on the big adventures . . . like me 'n' Erp here!"

"Yeah, like us guys," Erp said in between his deep raspy giggles. "None o' that sissy Gades ub Widzdum stuff. No sirrreee."

Kris was disappointed. If the Gates of Wizzdom were *sissy stuff*, then the whole game was ruined.

"Now, now, lad. Don't go gettin' all sad and sore and what. Erp 'n me would be jolly delighted to have you join up with us. And it's a right sharper deal than yours, lad. . . ." Derrick leaned over and whispered into Kris's ear, "We're after *hidden treasure!*"

"HIDDEN TREASURE!" shouted Kris, imagining pirate maps and giant caves and all sorts of ancient swords and things.

"SHHHHHHHH!" hissed Derrick slapping his hand over Kris's mouth. He glanced around quickly as if expecting spies to leap out of the bushes. "Mum lad! Keep it mum!"

He hurried Kris into the shadows looking very serious and secretive. Then he continued on.

"This ain't no sissy stuff, laddy. It's a pow'rful dangerous secret, this Hidden Treasure business! There's folks out there that ain't to be trusted lad.

You gotta be on your guard, see? You gotta watch yer backside . . . and stick close to me 'n Erp here!"

"Yeah," Erp whispered hoarsely. "Stick close t' us."

Derrick drew Kris under his arm and off they went, scurrying deep into the shadowy hills as if fleeing from some impending danger. It felt wonderfully adventurous to Kris. Much more adventurous than the Gates of Wizzdom and that sort of thing.

4
The Chess King's Treasure

Kris had followed his new companions for miles and miles, and they had gone over the strangest land a person could imagine. All the colorful hills had disappeared behind them, and only a few islands of bushes stuck up out of the smooth, flat ground. Stranger yet, the ground had turned into an endless floor of black and white squares. It felt as if they were traveling across the world's most enormous chessboard.

Derrick suddenly gestured for Kris and Erp to be quiet. He made them get down on their hands and knees, and the three of them snuck up behind a long hedge that had been pruned to look like a wall. Carefully, they peeked over the top of the hedge. There, on the other side of the bushes, stood two rows of Chess People. All of them (except the Pawns) were taller than Kris, and they were all moving about and whispering to one another in very important voices. The two Rooks stood at attention from inside little turrets that were strapped to their shoulders. The Knights trotted to and fro on little hobbyhorses that snorted and whinnied and, despite having no hoofs, kicked up dust as they stomped around. The Bishops were dressed in wonderful purple robes with golden tassels dangling all about. And the White King and Queen each sat proudly upon a sparkling, silver throne.

The King was busily signing documents and figuring tax tables and making laws, which the Pawns all passed among themselves saying, "Yes-yes! Hmmm, of course. Good law! Very good law!" And when the last Pawn was handed a parchment, he would shuffle off the board and drop it onto a stack of old laws and documents. (And since this had been going on for countless years, there was a very large pile.)

Kris was still watching this with great fascination when Derrick yanked him down behind the wall again.

"Alrighty, lad . . . here's your part in the adventure!" Derrick whispered. Kris perked up anxiously. "Did you see that shiny box that's sittin' under the King's chair?"

Kris nodded.

"Guess what, chum?" Derrick hissed with a devious smile. "That lovely, little box is full o' gold! That's right lad, gold and jewels and gems and lovely, lovely riches! It's just sittin' there gettin' all dusty, not doin' anybody a lick o' good. And I think it's a sad and awful pity, lad. A sad and awful pity! Ain't it a pity, Erp?"

"Yup, sure is a piddy," groaned Erp.

"So, here's the deal," Derrick continued. "Me 'n' Erp had the wondrous joy of findin' the treasure, so we thinks it's only fair to let you be the one to go out there and snatch it!"

"Snatch it?" said Kris. "You mean . . . like . . . take it?"

"Right, lad! Snatch it! Nab it! Grab it!" Derrick beamed with enthusiasm. "Easy as cream pie! You just sneaks up from behind and—"

"No way!" Kris broke in crossly. "That's just like stealin'!"

"I knowed he was gonna be a chicken!" Erp sneered, shaking his head.

"I'm NOT a chicken!" Kris said, trying to shout in a whisper. "But I don't steal, either!" He stepped up to Erp with his fists raised for combat. Erp loomed over him like a mountain, staring down at Kris dumbly.

"Uh-oh, he's gonna hit me!" Erp teased. "Hope I don't get scratched by his chicken claws! Ayuck-yuck-yuck!"

"Now, now, lads!" Derrick stepped between them. "No need for quarrels! We're all gentlemen

36

here." He turned to Kris and put his arm around his shoulder. "Look here, lad. There's an easy way to prove that you ain't a chicken . . . and without havin' to steal nothin', either. All you got to do is sneak out there and pluck the Treasure Chest out from under the chair, just to prove you ain't afraid to do it!"

"And then I put it back?" Kris added, still glaring at Erp.

"Preeeeecisely!" said Derrick with a big smile. "You picks it up real high in the air (so's to show how brave you are) and when we gives you the signal, you puts it back!"

"Okay," Kris gave in. "Just to prove it to that big dope!"

Erp smiled down at him showing his one, big tooth.

As quietly as possible, Kris squeezed through the miserable wall of bushes. His bare arms got some nasty scratches from thorns and bristly twigs, but he managed not to groan or shout. When he finally popped out of the bushes, he was only a few steps behind the King's throne. Fortunately, no one was looking in his direction at the time, so Kris crawled up to the Royal Court on his hands and knees.

The Treasure Chest was quite heavy for such a small box, which made it even more difficult to keep quiet while dragging it out from under the throne. If not for all of the chattering among the White Chess Court, Kris surely would have been heard. But he

managed to pull it out of its hiding place, and hoist it high in the air. He smiled proudly as his companions waved at him from behind the hedge.

Kris had just turned to put the treasure chest back under the King's chair when Derrick suddenly shouted from the bushes, "THIEF! THIEF!"

Kris, not knowing what else to do, hid the chest behind his back and stood up quickly. Every Chess Person in the entire White Court turned around to see what was happening. The King and Queen leered down at Kris over the backs of their chairs.

"What are you doing back there, boy?!" the King demanded.

"N-n-nothing, sir," Kris lied desperately. "Honest!"

"I don't trust him, Thadeus!" squawked the Queen. "He's a spy! That's what I say!" She stood up in her chair and screamed with deafening fury, "Guards! Have the boy interrogated this instant!"

None of the Chess Guards moved; the Queen was known for her rash orders, and no one was quite sure what to do.

"What do you have behind your back?" the King continued.

"Me?" Kris squeaked, looking around nervously. "Nothin' . . . really . . . just my hands, that's all."

"Do you wish to have him thrown into the dungeon, sire?" inquired a large White Knight.

"Yes, yes!" shouted the Queen. "He's probably got diseases! Take him away!"

Just then Derrick and Erp jumped out of the bushes and started shouting. "RUN FOR IT LAD!" screamed Derrick.

Kris took advantage of the sudden diversion and raced for an escape.

The White Chess Army was so badly confused by all this commotion that they ran about in all directions, crashing into one another violently.

"After them!" commanded the King. "They've stolen the Royal Treasure!"

"My diamonds!" screeched the Queen. "The scoundrels have stolen my precious diamonds! Lock them up! Dangle them from their toes!"

The bumbling White Army finally gathered its wits and charged across the chessboard in pursuit of the three thieves. Even so, their attack was horribly clumsy, with a great deal of clanking and stumbling and tripping, and a general uncertainty about which direction they were charging. (They had never been called to an actual military duty before.)

Derrick and Erp, on the other hand, were quite experienced in these matters. With Kris and the Treasure Chest pinched between them, they raced ahead of the angry Chess Army, changed directions behind a cluster of bushes, and ran all the way to the edge of the chessboard. Then, at the top of a long, steep hill, they slipped into the bramble and hid quietly. Derrick kept his hand over Kris's mouth until he was sure of their safety. In a few moments, the clattering and stumbling of Chess Men could be heard passing by. And in a few moments more, the thieves were safe.

Derrick carefully rose up out of the bushes and looked around to assure that they were in the clear. Then, squatting back down, he snatched the Treasure Chest out of Kris's hands and threw open the lid. It was glowing with jewels of every sort. Derrick's eyes swelled with pleasure.

"Beeeeeautiful!" Derrick gloated. "Lovely, lovely gems!"

"Ooooooo! Those is purty ones," added Erp.

Kris was still gasping and panting and trying to figure out everything that had just happened. He wasn't feeling too well right then.

"Well, lad!" said Derrick turning to Kris. "It looks like our little adventure is over! It's time for us to go our separate ways, right Erp?!"

Erp laughed wickedly. He reached down with one enormous hand and swept Kris up off the ground. "Bye-bye, little boy!"

"Wait a minute!" screamed Kris, dangling in the air.

"So long, Laddy. It's been mighty nice workin' with ya!" Derrick chuckled. "Off with him, Erp!"

And with one gentle toss, Erp sent Kris bouncing and bounding down the hillside like a little toy doll. He fell and he fell, rolling and tumbling, sliding and somersaulting, until finally he landed with a hard, nasty SMACK right in the middle of the Path to Mount Wizzdom.

5

A Speedy Gift from the Jack-of-All-Trades

Kris lay on his back in the center of the Pathway feeling more foolish than he'd ever felt in his life. How had he fallen for such obvious trickery? All in a few minutes time, he'd been taken in by a pair of thugs, tricked into criminal activities, and bounced down a hill like a rubber ball.

As if that wasn't enough, he'd landed on the Pathway right back where he'd started. Directly above his head were the same two signs:

The Path to Mount Wizzdom

which pointed down the proper trail, and

Shortcut

which pointed down the path that had gotten him

into this terrible mess. The more he sat there and thought about it, the more foolish he felt. So he stood up and dusted off his clothes and picked the leaves and twigs out of his hair.

Suddenly the Path began to glow beneath his feet. He jumped back quickly. The way things had been going lately, Kris was expecting something to explode or jump out or do any sort of dramatic thing. But the Path just continued glowing brighter and brighter, until finally, five words appeared. They said:

Draw One Dodo Bird Card

"Draw one Dodo Bird Card?" said Kris. And he looked around for something that might fit that description.

"POP!" came a loud noise from beside the Path, and a stack of enormous blue cards appeared. Kris stepped up to them cautiously. Sure enough, the word *Dodo* was written on the top card, so Kris decided he'd better take one.

It was about the size of a sheet of plywood and nearly as heavy. Kris stumbled and struggled to get the giant card off the pile. Then, balancing it on top of his head, he hauled it off the Path and rested it against a tree. He stepped back to examine the card and found himself staring at a picture of a five-foot-tall Dodo Bird (a big, cartoony creature with an orange beak and crossed eyes). It looked so silly that Kris felt inclined to giggle, when all of a sudden the

picture burst into life and the huge blue Bird came leaping out on top of him.

"Whaaaaahoooooo!" squawked the Dodo, zooming around Kris like a spastic boomerang. "Boy are *you* a Dodo Bird! Never should've left the Path to Mount Wizzdom! Lying, stealing, r-r-r-rotten friends!" He cackled and hooted and spoke so quickly that Kris could barely understand him.

"And what did you get for it all?!" the Bird shrieked as it fluttered up and stuck its beak in Kris's face. "Bumps and bruises! Whaaaaaahoooo! You'll never get to the Gates of Wizzdom that way! Keep up the bad work, dum-dum! Waaahoooohooooo!" And the giant Dodo hurled itself through the air, turned a clumsy back flip, and landed back inside the card in the same silly position it had started in.

Kris stood there for a moment, quite speechless. The Bird didn't move.

With great caution, he stepped up and touched the picture of the motionless Dodo. It still didn't move.

"Weird," said Kris and he stepped back onto the Pathway (taking frequent glances over his shoulder to be sure that the Bird was staying put).

Kris had lost a lot of time and made a lot of mistakes, so now he had to hurry. The Dodo was right and Kris knew it. He was never going to make it to Mount Wizzdom the way he'd been going. Mr. Weatherfield had warned him about tricks along the way; the Arrows had told him to stay on the Pathway; and now Kris had earned his first Dodo Bird Card. Two more cards and he'd lose the game. How humiliating!

"But nobody's perfect," thought Kris. "Anybody would've done the same stuff. Now I know what to look out for. It'd be impossible to trick me now!" He resigned himself to that attitude and marched down the Pathway as fast as he could walk.

It went along just as pleasantly as before, with colorful trees and flowers lining the Pathway, and a sky full of birds and butterflies. Mount Wizzdom climbed up into the clouds far off in the distance.

Kris hurried along trying to guess how long it

would take him to reach the mountain. If he were only allowed thirty minutes to finish the whole game, he mustn't have much time left. But somehow, it seemed as if time moved at a different speed inside Hoomania. In fact, it seemed as if he'd been there for hours. Maybe he was already late! Maybe he'd lost and he was stuck inside this game forever! Just then he remembered that he had his combination yo-yo/glow-in-the-dark watch in his pocket. He pulled it out in a hurry but found that it wasn't much help.

The hour hand and the minute hand were both spinning around like tiny propellers, but going in opposite directions. Meanwhile, the second hand was bouncing back and forth and going nowhere. "This sure is a weird place," Kris thought, and he put the watch back in his pocket.

While Kris had been busy worrying about the time, the Path had climbed a tall, bushy hill. And as he came to the top of this hill, he looked up and came to a sudden stop. What he saw was wonderful! No . . . it was beyond wonderful! It was absolutely the most superwonderful thing he'd ever seen.

It was sitting on a silver platform in the middle of the Pathway, and Kris instantly knew that it was a Rocket Car. Not just a run-of-the-mill Rocket Car, but a shiny, red, mega-turbo, all-terrain Rocket Car. One with a big, glass bubble over the cockpit and giant thruster rockets poking out on every side. He ran up to it and stuck his face against the glass bubble. It had gadgets everywhere! Shifters and levers and switches and lights . . . and Kris was hoping that he might be allowed to sit inside it, or better yet, go for a ride!

He started walking around back to look at the thrusters, when he tripped over something and tumbled to the ground. A big flat thing slid out from under the Rocket Car and stood up on end. It looked like a giant card, but when it spun around, Kris found himself looking at a person . . . or a picture of a person that stared back at him and frowned. The person looked exactly like the Jack in a deck of cards, except he was wearing work overalls and holding a monkey wrench.

"Aha, there you are! Late of course!" said the man checking his watch. Then he reached down and helped Kris up. "I'm Jack, the Jack-of-All-Trades. I'm the handyman around Hoomania. I do all the fixing, building, that sort of thing. So what do you think? Like it?" He pointed to the Rocket Car.

"Is it yours?" said Kris, hoping he'd get to sit in it.

"Nope," replied Jack, wiping off the smudge Kris had left on the glass bubble. "It goes with the game. And it's your turn champ!"

"You mean . . . I get to drive it?!" gasped Kris.

"You're playing the game aren't you?"

Kris nodded eagerly.

"Then you get to drive it! Hop in." Jack stepped aside.

The bubble over the cockpit suddenly raised, and

Kris climbed inside before you could snap your fingers. In no time, he was wearing a silver racing helmet and a pair of driving gloves, and the Rocket Car roared to a start.

"This is no ordinary car, kid," Jack instructed. "This little monster has a five-speed turbo with cruise control for driving on the Path, and a twin-jet inboard for when you get to the river."

Kris was busy playing with levers and things.

"Hey, are you listening, kid?" Jack tapped his shoulder.

"Huh?" Kris looked up from under the bulky helmet. "Oh . . . yeah . . . the Path and the river . . . right!"

"Right," Jack continued. "She's programmed to follow the Path straight to the river. At the end of the river, she'll take you right through the tunnels, and drive straight up Mount Wizzdom fast and safe! All you've gotta do is push the gas pedal, got it?"

"Sure, sure," said Kris racing the engine. "Can I go now?"

"I'm not kidding, kid. If you take this machine off the Path, you'll end up in *big* trouble. Got it? *Big* trouble!"

"Okay," said Kris. "I better go now. . . . See ya later!" And he slammed the cockpit bubble shut. He shoved the shift stick into gear, squished the gas pedal to the floor, and in one big cloud of smoke, disappeared down the Path to Mount Wizzdom in the hottest machine in the world!

It was the most fun Kris could ever remember having. The Rocket Car was fast and smooth and just his size. The colorful hillsides whizzed by outside his window, and the looming mass of Mount Wizzdom grew closer and closer as he sped towards it.

Kris was grown up now—he was driving. It was just like he always thought it would be. He could go anywhere. . . . He was free! Feeling so much freedom inspired him to go a little faster, and he pushed a little harder on the gas pedal.

Off to the left, Kris thought he saw a quick flash of colored light flicker by. For some reason, it caught his interest, so he stepped on the brakes. The rocket car stopped instantly. Kris threw it into reverse and backed up for a short ways.

Sure enough, on the left side of the Path there was a big, round tunnel with bright lights flashing from somewhere inside. Above the Tunnel's entrance was a sign, also in flashing lights. It read:

Pinball Boulevard

"Hmmm, Pinball Boulevard," Kris said to himself. "It goes off the Path . . . but it's just a Boulevard. Maybe I could just go a little ways, then turn around." The engine idled loudly as if telling Kris to get moving. "Aw . . . just a peek won't hurt," Kris resolved, and he turned the rocket car into the opening.

It was a wonderful Tunnel. Lights of every color

were flashing on and off. Loud, crazy music was playing (it sounded something like a carnival). And from inside the Rocket Car, Kris felt like the most adventurous person in the whole world.

As the Tunnel went along, it became narrower. The music continued, but the flashing lights fell behind him. Soon, it was nearly pitch black and Kris was thinking that he'd better turn around before he bumped into something. But a little circle of flashing light up ahead caught his curiosity. He approached it slowly.

It turned out to be a big archway, and when Kris turned to go through it, he found himself overlooking the strangest, most amazing valley you could ever imagine. It was a wide, flat land filled with colored lights and musical noises. But surrounding the entire valley was a tall, smooth wall covered with glowing shapes and bright colors. At the far end was a giant scoreboard lit up in glowing numbers. And all across the floor below, there were flashing lights shaped like shooting stars; there were buzzing buzzers and ringing bells; there were things that looked like giant mushrooms (but with rubber edges); there were huge swirls of glowing color shaped like tornadoes and explosions.

In a few moments, Kris realized that he was actually looking out over an enormous pinball machine. Not just a big pinball machine—but one the size of his neighborhood! He gasped with delight, and wondered how one would play such an enor-

50

mous game.

He didn't have to wonder about that for long, though. Because, just then the scoreboard lit up with bright red words that said:

Begin Play!

And directly after that, out from behind him came a low, rumbling noise . . . something like the sound of a bowling ball rolling down a lane. Kris turned around just in time to see a ball bearing the size of a boulder coming his way at a tremendous speed. In a terrified panic, he shifted into gear and slammed down on the gas peddle. But it was too late. The ball bearing smacked the Rocket Car with a terrible THWACK!!! and sent it hurling through the air like a tiny pebble.

At a frightening speed, the Rocket Car flew into the flashing maze of lights and flickers and chiming bells, and was soon being tossed about like a regular pinball.

Helplessly, the little car shot from bumper to bumper. It was flicked off flickers, bounced off bouncers, battered, tumbled, swatted, and rolled. The noises got louder and the score got higher, and poor Kris was beginning to feel like a human beanbag. All he could hear was crumbling metal and ringing bells. All he could see was a blur of color and the explosive flashing of lights. Finally, with one mighty FLINK! a big, silver flicker sent Kris and the Rocket Car shooting out the exit tunnel.

Down the chute he went, rumbling against the tunnel walls, thundering downhill at a terrifying speed. Then, out into the air he flew! The little car spiraled through the sky like a poorly thrown football. Down it went, spouting smoke and throwing broken pieces every which way. Kris screamed helplessly, covered his eyes, and CRASHHHHH!, landed in the top of a big, bushy tree.

6
Kris Learns How to Row

It was a good while before Kris could get his wits about him. He unsnapped his helmet and pulled it from his pounding head. That helped. But still, the world seemed to be reeling around much too fast, and his ears were ringing with all sorts of *beeps* and *clanks* and *thwacks* and *dings*.

He leaned out of the crumbled cockpit to figure out where he was, and the side of the Rocket Car gave way. Kris plunged down through a big nest of twigs and branches, and landed on his bottom on the ground. He wondered how much more of this he could take. Up above him, in the top of the tree, the Rocket Car's twisted motor coughed and sputtered its last few gasps, and finally died.

"Oh, great," moaned Kris. "Now I've done it."

He knew quite well that he'd failed to follow his orders and had probably ruined any hope of winning the game. So he sat there on the grass beneath the wreckage of the Rocket Car with his face in his hands, while little pieces of machinery dropped to the ground all around him.

"POP!" came a loud noise from behind Kris. He turned around just in time to see a stack of giant blue cards appear.

Kris was just wondering if he shouldn't run, when "POP!" came a second noise . . . and up went one of the giant cards, with a big pair of yellow feet coming out from beneath it!

"POP!" it went again, and the card went flying off into the bushes as the flapping, fluttering, screeching Dodo Bird rushed through the air towards Kris.

"Waaaaaahoooooeeeyyyy!!!" the Bird screamed. It did a backward somersault and landed on Kris's lap. "A *fool* and his Rocket Car are soon parted! *Fools* despise wisdom and instruction! *Fools* are big headed and careless!" (It pinched Kris's face between its two blue wings.) "Does that sound like anybody *youuu* know?"

And suddenly, the Dodo was up again. It did three consecutive cartwheels, squawked in Kris's ear, "*Keep up the blunders, Brain Boy!!!*" and then disappeared back into the stack of Dodo Cards.

The world was silent again.

"What good is that ridiculous Bird," thought Kris. "Now I've lost the game and I'll never get to Mount

Wizzdom and I'm probably stuck here forever. I've lost, and all that stupid Bird does is pick on me. Who cares?" And Kris went back to pouting, with his face planted firmly in the palms of his hands.

At the foot of the hill on which Kris was sitting and pouting, there was a river. And on that river there was a big boat shaped like a fish. And the Captain of that boat was standing on the deck and staring at Kris through a telescope at that very moment. He'd seen what had happened with the Rocket Car (and quite frankly, he had rather expected it!). So, knowing his duty well, he put his telescope aside and called out in a loud, salty voice, *"All aboooard for Mount Wizzdom!"*

Kris jumped up instantly, looking around for the voice.

"The Boat to Mount Wizzdom leaves in two minutes!" came a second cry.

This time Kris spotted the Captain. He was standing on board the strange boat that was docked at the foot of the hill. And leading right up to the boat was the colorful Pathway to Mount Wizzdom. It followed the hillside right down to the dock where the fish-shaped boat was moored, and then it disappeared underwater. Kris raced down the hill with renewed hope and crossed the wooden dock just as the Captain was pulling in his anchor.

"Wait! Wait!" Kris screamed. "Wait for me! I'm goin' to Mount Wizzdom!" And he leaped from the dock to the fish-shaped boat, dropping onto a seat cushion with a relieved sigh.

The old Captain looked down at him and raised one of his fluffy grey eyebrows.

It was then that Kris noticed that the Captain was an Ant! A huge Ant (the size of Kris's father), but he had a fuzzy, grey beard and was wearing a seaman's uniform. Kris was startled and fell off his seat, getting himself tangled up in a net. The Captain reached down with three hands and pulled Kris back onto the cushion.

"No lyin' around on this boat, lad!" laughed the Captain in a deep, raspy voice. "This doesn't look like a Rocket Car, now does it? You've got to *row* your way to Mount Wizzdom!" Then he let out a long, jolly chuckle, slapped Kris on the back, and set him on a seat between two oars. The Captain moved to the stern and took his position at the rudder.

"But . . . I don't know how to row," Kris protested.

"Then now's the time for learnin', matey! The Gates o' Wizzdom will be closin' soon!"

Kris pulled back on the oars, and the fish-shaped boat slid out into the river. Since he'd never rowed before, he was pretty sloppy at first. But with a few instructions from the Captain, and a little bit of practice (which he got lots of that day), Kris was rowing like a regular boatman.

Before long, he was almost enjoying himself. And before much longer, he had nearly forgotten that he

was rowing at all. He rythmically pulled the oars
back, leaned forward, pulled back, and so forth, as
the Captain sang songs about ships and oceans and
storms. Most of these songs were funny, which
helped take Kris's mind off the work of rowing. The
one he liked best went like this:

There was a lad who had a skiff,
And Binkers was his name.
He took it out across the riff
And on the waters tame.

He rowed himself across the weeds
And landed on the Isle
He set his hammock 'tween two trees
And thought he'd nap awhile.

But o'er the hills the sky grew mean
And turned to smoky black.
Binkers saw the distant storm
But thought he'd not turn back.

"I've come to nap, and nap I shall!"
Said Binkers where he set.
"I'll sleep a bit and then row back,
Long before I'm wet."

But when he closed his little eyes
The storm clouds gathered 'round.
And by the time that Binkers woke
The rain was pouring down.

Binkers hurried to his skiff
And took his oars in hand.
He battled 'cross the swelling splash
Toward the distant land.

Over tipped his little boat
And overboard he fell
Losing all his fishin' rigs
And both his oars as well.

Binkers barely made it back,
He'd had a nasty dunk.
But then he caught it from his dad
Because his skiff had sunk.

"My boy," said Binker's angry pop,
"You've learned a lesson great:
He who waits until the storm
Is waiting much too late."

"Observe the Ant, my foolish son,
He works before it rains—
He covers up his little holes
Or else they'd all be drains!"

Two or three songs later, Kris was beginning to feel tired. Tiredness soon turned to soreness, and rowing soon ceased being any fun at all. "I'm gettin' kind of tired," said Kris, hoping the Captain would take the oars.

"I'd like to help you out lad," said the Captain, looking quite sympathetic. "But I'm afraid this is what comes from smashin' that Rocket Car. When you make things harder for yourself, you've got to pay the price. If somebody stepped in and carried your load for you all the time . . . why, you'd never learn a thing, now would ya?"

"All this work just 'cause I made one little mistake," whined Kris.

"Har! Har! Har!" the Captain burst into loud, raspy laughter. "One little mistake, eh?! Lad, yer a whole bundle o' mistakes! It's not gonna get any easier for you until you've learned how to do some swifter thinkin'. This little bit o' work here will help you remember: makin' the right choices is always a bit o' work!" And the Captain gave Kris a good swat on the back as he laughed his hearty laugh.

Kris realized that unfortunately the Captain was right. He was in trouble a good deal too often, and usually it was because he didn't stop to think. Just like that kid, Binkers, in the song. Well, maybe he could take rowing for just a little while longer.

"But cheer up, boy!" the Captain continued. "Why don't you turn yerself around and look what's ahead."

Kris turned in his seat and, as he did, the Captain shouted, *Land Hooooooooo!*

Sure enough, straight ahead of the boat was a big cove set into the grassy foothills of Mount Wizzdom. Looming high into the clouds, but still a ways in the distance, stood the jagged mountain. For the first time, Kris could make out the colored stones of the Pathway climbing up the rocky mountainside.

61

"All right!" Kris cheered. "I made it! I could still win, huh?!"

"Indeed you could, lad," the Captain nodded.

Kris rowed heartily while staring over his shoulder at the nearing shoreline. The Captain steered the boat into the cove and up against a long dock. He threw a rope out catching a post on the dock; the boat jerked to a stop.

Kris looked around for the Pathway, but saw only sandy shorelines and the hulking shape of Mount Wizzdom in the background. "Where's the Path?" said Kris, anxious to get back on land.

The Captain pointed down into the water.

Kris leaned overboard and, sure enough, there along the river floor went the colored Pathway.

"But . . . where's it go?" he asked.

"Yer not done rowin' yet, my boy," said the Captain with a smile, and he pointed to the far end of the cove.

Indeed, there at the water's edge was a cavern going into the hillside, and above it was a sign that read:

Tunnel to Mount Wizzdom

"Neato!" Kris gasped. "We're goin' into that Tunnel?"

"Now listen close, matey," the Captain continued on. "Here's where you put to practice this little rowin' lesson of yours. And I mean the part about thinkin' swifter and the like!"

Kris sat at attention as the Captain lowered a small dinghy from the stern into the water.

"That Tunnel over there leads to Mount Wizzdom. It's really the Pathway; it's just yer floatin' over it instead of walkin'. The main thing is, you've got to follow the right Tunnel! It's plain and clear. . . . There's signs all the way. You'll be takin' this little dinghy here. You just keep yer head about you and make yer choices with some thinkin'!"

"You're not coming?" said Kris with surprise.

"Sorry lad, but you're on yer own from here. Just watch yerself this time! You've got no chances left, so don't go doin' anything foolish."

"Don't worry, Mr. Ant Captain, sir," said Kris. "This time, I'm not gonna get smashed up, or go off the right Path, or anything!"

"That's right, my boy!" the Captain smiled. "You just keep that attitude from now on. When you see the trouble comin', just remember: Think straight and stick with it! Now off you go!"

The Captain swept Kris out of his seat and gently dropped him into the little dinghy.

"One more thing," the Captain added. "There'll be some treats for you up on the side o' Mount Wizzdom—rewards for all yer hard work. Just remember that treats are fine and good . . . as long as you don't let 'em get in the way of what's really important. Just remember that it doesn't do you any good to be on the Path to Mount Wizzdom, if you're lyin' asleep in the middle of it! Now off to Mount

63

Wizzdom—and good luck to you lad!"

With a flick of his wrist, the Captain freed his anchor rope from the dock. He gave the oars one mighty haul and the fish-shaped boat soared out into open water as smoothly as a swan. Kris waved from his little dinghy as the Captain quickly sailed out of sight. He could hear the raspy voice singing a ballad in the distance.

Finally, he took his own oars in hand, and hurried towards the Tunnel that led to Mount Wizzdom.

7

A Run-in with
Pin-the-Tail Pirates

At first, traveling through the Tunnel had seemed like an exciting idea. It would be like an exploration. Kris imagined that he might even discover dinosaur bones or a secret world full of three-eyed cave people.

But once he actually got inside the Tunnel and realized that he was all alone, Kris decided he wasn't really in much of an exploring mood.

For one thing, the Tunnel was as black as coal, and Kris had never been very fond of the dark. He stayed so close to the rock wall that his oars clunked and banged against it constantly.

And for another thing, Kris began to realize that in the dark he had no idea what was ahead. He had no idea what *might* be underneath his boat. And with this sort of thinking, in the pitch black and the silence, it wasn't long before Kris was feeling pretty nervous.

So far, the nastiest creatures he had seen were those two awful characters, Derrick and Erp. But how was he to know that this dark, damp Tunnel wasn't full of Sea Serpents and Goblins and other slimy things?

Did something just move down by his feet?

Yes . . . he was sure it did. . . .

It was cold, and it was up against one of his feet now! It rocked back and forth against him as the boat moved.

Carefully, he took an oar out of the water and got ready to smash whatever it was over the head. But just then, *CRUNCH*, the boat collided with the cavern wall, and *CLANK*, the cold thing by his feet bumped against his shoe. It sounded like metal. He poked it with his oar. It was metal!

He reached down and picked it up and was much relieved to find that it was only a lantern.

He felt around until he located a knob. He turned it and the lantern lit up the cavern like a piece of the sun! He set it on the bow of the boat and rowed on into the Tunnel, feeling much more inclined toward adventure.

In a while, some lights appeared in the distance, along with them came a variety of noises such as laughter, music, and various banging sounds. Kris hurried toward them, and found that he had come to an underground village of some sort. Unfortunately, all of the lights and noises were coming out of little tunnels that went off to the side. These little tunnels were marked with signs that said things like:

**Musical Chairsville
This-a-Way!!!**

and

**Come One, Come All!
To the Jolly Joker's Arcade.**

As usual, Kris wanted very much to explore these places. But this time he was determined not to leave the Pathway (or Tunnel in this case), and he was quite determined to get to Mount Wizzdom. So he rushed himself along feeling quite pleased about his good sense.

After passing a good many such tunnels, all with flashing signs, the action came to an end and the Tunnel split in two. In one direction was a sign that said:

**This Way to PRIZE-O-RAMA!
Play Fun Games and Win Big Prizes!**

and above the other route was a sign that someone had tried to cover up with a blanket. The readable part looked like this:

is Way to

nt Wizzdom

It seemed quite clear to Kris what this second sign

said, but he wondered why someone had covered it up. Perhaps the Tunnel was closed? Or perhaps it was a trick. But, maybe there was something dangerous between there and Mount Wizzdom. Which way to go? Whom to trust?

From down the first opening, he could hear singing and laughter. There was music like merry-go-rounds, flashing lights, and the smell of popcorn and doughnuts. Someone was certainly having a great deal of fun down that way.

But down the dusky Tunnel to Mount Wizzdom, there was silence. Kris wasn't really afraid—he had his lantern—but it was not the more inviting route.

"Hmmm," Kris thought to himself. " 'Use yer head' . . . that's what Captain Ant said. And somebody covered up that sign . . . probably to trick me. That's what Derrick and Erp would've done. I'll just bet!"

So this time, Kris resolved to stay on the right Path . . . or at least to take the route that seemed most sensible. And if he got tricked this time, at least he'd know he'd done his best. Nonetheless, he approached carefully (as all wise people will do when they come to questionable territory). But his answer came immediately.

For, out of the other Tunnel, there arose a horrible ruckus. A whole mob of voices burst into shouting, and the loudest one bellowed, "GET 'IM LADS!!! He didn't fall fer it!"

Then, from around the corner came a hulking

boat, battered with scars. High on the center mast was a sail bearing the picture of a laughing skull. On board, screaming and laughing and shaking weapons in the air, were half a dozen of the ugliest creatures Kris had ever seen. Quite clearly, they were Pirates.

But these weren't regular Pirates—these were Pin-the-Tail Pirates, a band of Donkeys that had turned nasty and taken up robbery. Some had a steel hook instead of a front hoof; some had a patch over one eye; and all of them had their tails in the wrong places.

Kris got one look at them and hauled back on his oars with all his strength. His little boat wobbled and teetered as he hurried into the Tunnel to Mount Wizzdom.

But the horrible band of Pirates charged toward him at a much faster speed. With eight of them rowing, and the underground breeze filling their sail, it would not be long before the Pirate boat would overtake Kris. To make matters worse, they had a cannon on board. Soon big metal balls were blasting the water all around Kris's tiny boat. The barbaric Donkey Pirates roared with laughter as the water broke beneath their ship, gaining on Kris by the second.

Just then, the Pirate in the crow's nest let out a terrible howl and the main mast snapped in two, sending him crashing into the water. The monstrous boat reeled over onto one side, throwing Pirates

across the deck and nearly capsizing. In the thrill of their pursuit, the Pirates hadn't noticed the Tunnel ceiling dropping lower.

Kris let up on his oars, quite surprised by this sudden change of luck. He watched (with some delight) as three of the Donkey Pirates tumbled overboard into the river. The others clung to the boat in terror. Then, the great Pirate boat shook herself and stood upright again. Kris waited to see what would happen.

There was a moment's confusion on board—some banging and shouting—and in a moment something was being lowered off one side of the Pirate boat. Kris got a horrible feeling that he knew what it was, and he began rowing at full speed.

He hadn't gone far when his fears proved correct. A motor came roaring to a start from beside the wounded Pirate ship. And in another moment, a small motorboat was growling at top speed and headed in his direction.

In the glow of his lantern, he could see the little boat approaching from behind. There was nothing he could do. He was trapped and he couldn't understand why this was happening to him. He'd taken the proper Tunnel. He'd made the wise decision as everyone was always telling him to do. And now everything was going all wrong.

" 'Use yer head,' " said Kris, trying to keep faith. " 'Think straight and stick with it!' That's what Captain Ant said. . . ."

The motorboat screamed up in front of him, cutting him off, and the next thing Kris knew, he was staring into the ugly faces of three Pin-the-Tail Pirates. They were holding croquet mallets and pool sticks and waving them around like swords. The Pirate Captain leaned over onto Kris's boat and smiled eerily.

"Alrighty little mate! You done caused us a nasty bit o' trouble! How abouts you hands over all o' yer loot right NOW!!!"

The other two laughed the way only Donkey Pirates can laugh.

"But . . . I don't have any loot," said Kris, quite honestly.

"C'mon skipper! Don't give us that!" the evil Captain persisted.

"Honest. . . ." Kris insisted. "Look . . . I'll prove it." He emptied his pockets onto the boat seat. All he had was his combination yo-yo/watch, a pack of soggy gum, and a nickel.

"Arrrrrgh!" growled the Donkey Captain, scooping up the meager treasures. "No matter. You'll fetch a good price down in the Checker Mines! Right boys?" His comrades laughed raucously, and it made them sound even dumber than they looked.

Kris didn't know what this Checker Mines place was all about. But if the Pirates were going to take him there, he knew it couldn't be good, and it certainly wouldn't get him to the top of Mount Wizzdom. So he needed a plan . . . and quick!

72

The Donkey Captain reached over to grab Kris, but Kris pulled away.

"Excuse me, sir," he squeaked nervously. "But shouldn't your Captain be taking care of this kind of stuff?"

"Whattaya mean?" screamed the Pirate. "I *am* the Captain! Now get over here ya little—"

"Why should I believe that you're the Captain when you've got your tail pinned onto your neck?" said Kris, dodging the Pirate's hook and feeling lots bolder. "It looks pretty dumb, you know. Besides, that guy over there looks a *lot* more piratey than you! And his tail's closer to where it's supposed to be."

"Who, Rufus? Har-har-har!" laughed the Pirate Captain. "Rufus ain't got the brains of a mushroom! Why he'd never be able to—"

But the Captain couldn't finish. Rufus thumped him on the back of the head with his croquet mallet. The Captain tumbled overboard with a loud splash and disappeared.

"HAR! I'll gib ya mutchroooom!" Rufus growled toothlessly.

"Hey! Why'd ya do that for, ya dum bloke?!" shouted the third Pirate, a tall scruffy fellow wearing five gold earrings.

"I ain't no dum doke!" Rufus snarled back and leaped on top of his comrade.

They kicked and bit and put on such a thrashing brawl that they nearly capsized the motorboat. On and on it went. Hair went flying, boards were broken, and horrible filthy words were uttered. Finally, when both of them were hanging over one edge of the boat, Kris leaned over and gave it a little tip. Over they went! Both of the Pirates toppled out into the water where they instantly got soggy and sunk. (Because they were Pin-the-Tail Pirates, and they were made completely out of paper.)

Kris grabbed his oars and was about to bolt out of there (just in case some more Pirates were about). But suddenly it occurred to him: there was an empty motorboat sitting in the water right beside him! So he snatched his lantern and his oars, and moved into the Pirate's motorboat. The motor started on the first try, and soon Kris was cruising in luxury down the Tunnel to Mount Wizzdom.

"Thanks a lot, Pirates!" Kris shouted, waving back at the battered Pirate Ship.

But no one heard him. They were all fighting about who was to blame for everything.

8

A Short Stay at a Long Feast

Kris sped through the Tunnel as quickly as the little boat would allow. It turned out to be a rather long journey, and it would've been an exhausting one if not for the Pirates' little motorboat. But after miles and miles of curving and dipping and winding about in the darkness, the underground river suddenly turned a corner and spilled out into open daylight. The Tunnel had come to an end.

What a beautiful sight it was! The stream poured out into a big, green pond with lilies and cattails growing round the shoreline. It took a moment for Kris's eyes to adjust to the bright sunlight, so he turned off the motor and rested in the middle of the pond for a while.

Soon he noticed a sign on a far bank of the pond:

To the Gates of Mount Wizzdom

At the foot of the signpost, the colored Pathway emerged from the water and started going across land again. It crossed the shore and climbed straight up the side of the great mountain until it looked like a tiny strip of ribbon near the top. At the mountain's very peak was a castle. It looked awfully tiny sitting so far up in the sky, but Kris could tell that it was going to be magnificent. He could just barely make out the crystal Gates from where he sat.

"I'm almost there," thought Kris. But it looked like a terribly long climb.

Indeed, it was a tiresome climb. The Path went straight as a line right up the side of Mount Wizzdom. There were no twists and no cutbacks. This often meant climbing up ledges that Kris would've preferred not to climb. But there were always good footholds and handholds in the cracks between the colored stones. So, with a great deal of sweating and panting, Kris picked his way up the side of Mount Wizzdom and slowly drew closer to the crystal Gates at the top.

This Path had one very annoying habit. Every ledge looked as if it led to the top of the mountain. Kris would anxiously struggle his way up each cliff certain that it would be the last. But then, when he reached the top of one ledge, he'd find himself standing at the bottom of another one. This went on and on, until Kris had climbed at least seven respectable cliffs. He was losing hope quickly. His strength was nearly gone, he was getting hungry, and every part of his body was tired and sore.

After two more such ledges, he was beginning to doubt that he would ever reach the top. Perhaps this was all just a horrible trick! Furthermore, Kris thought, what good does it do to work so hard and never get anywhere? The longer he dwelt on this thought, the angrier and wearier he became, until, finally, he resolved that he would get to the top of one last ledge and quit!

With that decision made, he gathered up enough strength to climb a few more yards to the top of the cliff. Then, he tumbled onto a flat landing at the top of the ledge and lay on his back gasping and groaning. With his eyes aimed straight up in the air, he could see the shining Gates of Mount Wizzdom high above him. They looked a good deal closer than before, but it still looked like a long hike. Too long of a hike for him, anyway.

Lying there on his back, Kris suddenly thought he could smell something baking . . . something like cake or pie. He sat up quickly, hoping this was true, and what he saw made him jump to his feet!

All around him, in a wide valley, was a land full of wonderful treats. Edible treats! They were growing out of the mountainside like a forest of goodies. There were hills made of ice cream and lumps of cake growing like shrubbery. There were flower beds of lollipops, and rivers of sparkling fruit punch. There were gardens full of fruits and candies and every sort of wonderful food. It was much too good to be true, especially when Kris had become so tired and hungry.

He raced along grabbing every sort of goodie that grew alongside the Pathway. (Fortunately, he still had the good sense not to go off the Path!) He helped himself to handfuls of cake and bunches of grapes. He sipped juice from a blossom shaped like a tea cup. He gobbled down berries of all sorts of flavors. Before long he was feeling quite refreshed, and he decided not to give up on his trip to the Gates of Wizzdom after all.

Just as he was about to start on his way, he found himself between three little hills of ice cream. One was vanilla, one was strawberry, and one was chocolate. He thought he'd just have a taste of each before he started up the mountain again. But, when he went to take a scoop off the chocolate one, it turned around!

It had big lazy eyes and an enormous mouth that was very messy from eating all day. It opened its eyes just slightly, and Kris jumped back. It stared at him for a short while and, in the slowest, dullest voice Kris had ever heard, it said, "Sit doooooown and join the feeeeeeeast."

A bit shaken, Kris stepped backwards and bumped into the strawberry hill. This one also turned around. It had big rosy lips and dark eyelashes that sparkled with sugar. It spoke in the voice of a very tired, very lazy woman, "Rest up a little, darrrrrrling."

Kris stood between them, staring at them both. Finally, he realized that they weren't lumps of ice cream at all. They were big round creatures who had grown so large that they *looked* like lumps of ice cream. Finally, the vanilla one turned around.

"Relaaaaaaaaaaax," it said. "Have sumthin' to eeeeeeeeeeeeeat."

Indeed, they did look wonderfully comfortable and content. Each of them had a heap of goodies in each arm and another pile at its feet. They seemed to be sitting or lying down (you couldn't tell which) in big piles of whipped cream.

These creatures were Sluggards. At one time, they had each looked like a normal sort of Game Token. But after countless years in this land of goodies, they had grown enormously fat and had taken on the colors of their favorite flavors.

"Um . . . I'd sure love to stay," Kris said awkwardly, "but I gotta get goin' up to the Gates of Mount Wizzdom."

"Sloooooooow dowwwwwn boooyyy," said the Chocolate Sluggard.

Kris did feel just a bit like resting.

"Noooo hurryyyyyyyy, deeeeeeear," said the Strawberry Sluggard.

In fact, Kris's eyes felt a little heavy.

"Ressssssssst," said the Vanilla Sluggard.

"Eeeeeeeeeat."

Actually, a short nap sounded rather good. "Yes, that's a good idea," thought Kris as he sunk to the ground. "First a nap . . . then later on, a nice, big snack."

He stretched himself out onto the colored Path, yawning. The world became blurry; his head was groggy. Then, as softly as the sound of raindrops on grass, the Strawberry Sluggard began singing a lullaby . . . a lovely, soothing lullaby about clouds and birds and breezy days.

Slowly, silently, the Vanilla Sluggard reached out with a candy cane and hooked it around Kris's leg. As the world grew foggier and foggier, and Kris slipped closer and closer to sleep, the creature dragged Kris towards him . . . which would soon get him off the Path to Mount Wizzdom!

Kris could feel the ground moving underneath him, but it was all so very dreamlike. It was all flowing pictures and smells and wonderful flavors. He didn't want to wake from it; it was a marvelous, peaceful dream and he wanted to let it consume him and take away all his cares.

But, suddenly, from somewhere in the mixture of all those dreams, Kris imagined he could see the Ant Captain. He thought he could hear the old sailor shouting from the bow of his boat: "Just remember, lad, it doesn't do you any good to be on the right Pathway if you're lyin' asleep in the middle of it!" Kris stirred. He didn't like those words. They didn't

80

fit with the dream.

He tried to shake it off, but couldn't. Something was wrong. Something was horribly wrong!

Suddenly Kris sprang to his feet. He found himself at the very edge of the Pathway with an enormous candy cane wrapped around his knee. And there was the Vanilla Sluggard tugging at the other end of the stick, trying to pull Kris off the Path!

"Hey! Let me go!" screamed Kris.

"Relaaaaaaaaaax. . . ." groaned the Sluggard.

Kris snapped the candy cane in two with a sharp kick and turned to run away. But the Chocolate Sluggard blocked him with a giant lollipop, and the Strawberry one was trying to tie a loop of string licorice around him. Fortunately, they all moved so slowly that in no time Kris had freed himself and was racing up the Pathway.

"Cooooooooome baaaaaaaaack!" called the Chocolate Sluggard.

"Dooooon't goooooooooo. . . ." howled the Strawberry one.

"Staaaaaaaay . . . eeeeeeeeeat!" they all moaned in their deep, half-asleep voices. But it was too late—Kris was out of their reach and running toward the Gates of Wizzdom.

9

Inside the Gates of Wizzdom

Kris ran as fast as he could all the way through the strange valley full of treats and goodies. He had almost fallen for the Sluggards' tricks, and it had put quite a scare into him. He was determined to go straight to the Gates of Wizzdom now, running all the way, just so he couldn't get himself into any further trouble.

But suddenly, out of the air, fell a huge stack of giant cards. They landed smack in the middle of the Pathway in front of Kris. He thumped into them and bounced off onto the ground. The top card flew into the air, and out jumped the big, blue Dodo Bird screaming and fluttering like a lunatic.

"Yaaaaaahoooooooeeeeeey!" it howled, hopping toward Kris like a pogo stick.

But Kris jumped up to face it. "I didn't do anything!" he shouted angrily.

"I know!" the Dodo squawked, landing upside down on its wing tips. "I'm on my way to yell at the Sluggards!"

Then the Bird lunged into the air, spun around like a crashing airplane, and landed on one foot, with its beak in Kris's face. And in a quiet voice, it said, "But while I'm here . . . Congratulations!" Then, ZOOOOSH! It was gone.

Kris looked all around, but the Bird had completely disappeared.

Then, from back down the Path a ways, came a loud, ranting clatter. How the Dodo had gotten there, Kris had no idea, but he could hear the strange bird cackling and raving at the Sluggards.

"How long will you lie down, O Sluggard?!" squawked the Dodo.

"Forrrreverrrrrrrrr," came the drawling reply.

"A little sleep, a little slumber," the Dodo recited, "and your poverty will come upon you like a robber!"

"Somebody wanna hush that birrrrrrrrd."

"Like a door upon its hinges, the Sluggard turns upon its bed!"

It went on like this for quite some time, but Kris couldn't stick around to listen. For all of a sudden, the Timer Bell sounded its echoing ring. The Gates of Wizzdom were closing!

Kris raced up the Pathway in a terrible panic. As

the Pathway curved up the last towering pinnacle, he could see the drawbridge slowly raising towards the Gates of Mount Wizzdom.

Although the trail was painfully steep, Kris pressed on, determined to reach the drawbridge before it closed. He was almost there! But now the drawbridge was halfway closed. . . . And between the ground and the Castle was a terrible chasm, a deep gulf with sheer cliffs on either side. As the drawbridge raised towards the crystal Gates, the chasm grew wider and wider. Kris ran his fastest, hoping he could still jump and reach the drawbridge. But as he approached, he could see the horrible drop at the edge of the chasm. . . . It must've been miles deep! He knew he mustn't think about it. He ran the last few yards, gaining as much speed as he could, and then he leaped!

His fingers caught the edge of the drawbridge. He swung a foot over to the other side. Only a few feet of space were left—he only had a moment.

With the rest of his strength, he hurled his entire body over the edge of the drawbridge and slid down into the Castle behind the Gates of Mount Wizzdom.

For a moment, there was complete silence. The Castle was dark and empty. Kris sat on the ground waiting for something to happen.

Then instantly, a thousand chandeliers flashed on, filling the room with light. At the same moment,

a chorus of voices broke into cheers! And Kris found himself standing in the middle of an enormous crystal chamber surrounded by dozens of Game People (most of whom he had met on his journey).

The Ant Captain was there, so was the Jack-of-All-Trades. The Chess King and Queen were there along with all the Knights and Rooks and Bishops and so forth. They all raced towards Kris shouting congratulations of every sort. He was very glad to see them all, especially the Ant Captain, and it looked like there was going to be some sort of party in his honor!

Just then a troop of Chessmen blew their trumpets.

The sound echoed several times throughout the crystal chamber, and the crowd of Game People began to back away toward the walls. Kris stood in the middle of the room looking quite confused.

A Knight holding a long paper scroll cried out: "Hear Ye, O Hear Ye, All Citizens of Hoomania, the Principality of Wizzdom, and All Various Parts of the Non-Game World. Announcing his Royal Feathership, the Great, the Magnificent, the World Renowned . . . Solomon Owl!"

With that, the Knight stepped aside pointing to a platform high up the chamber wall. The crowd applauded with marvelous enthusiasm; all eyes were fixed on the crystal platform.

In a moment, a sort of scratching and shuffling sound could be heard. The applauding grew louder.

And in another moment, a large brown owl with bushy, white eyebrows stepped onto the platform from a hidden side door. The cheering shook the chamber. This was Solomon Owl.

The great bird stood silently for a while peering out over his audience calmly. Then, he raised both wing tips just slightly, and jumped from the platform out into open air. He spun around once, dropped straight towards the floor, and stopped himself abruptly with a gentle snap of his wings. His feet touched the floor silently, and he completed his landing with a lovely pirouette.

The crowd once again burst into cheers as they huddled around the honorable Owl. Solomon bowed once, then lifted a wing and the room became dead silent. Then, as if rehearsed, the Game People stepped away from the Owl forming a path between him and Kris.

Solomon Owl hobbled towards Kris slowly. He stepped up in front of the boy and looked him firmly in the eyes.

"Are Yooooou the Kristopher Atwood who enters Wizzdom?" said the Owl in a sudden and owlish sort of voice.

"Yes, sir!" Kris answered proudly.

"You are!?" the Owl hooted, surprised by Kris's boldness. "Well, goodness gracious!"

"Yes, sir, Mr. Owl," Kris continued, smiling his brightest. "Does this mean I won the game?!"

"Won the game? Won the game?" Solomon took

off his big, round glasses and wiped them with a
hanky. "Well . . . dear . . . hmmm. I think we shall
have to engage in a Brief Review." A loud gasp
spread among the crowd.

"A review?" said Kris, expecting perhaps a prize
or something.

"Yes, a Brief Review. Uh . . . in Poetic Form, of
course," the Owl added.

"O goodie! A poem, a poem!" chanted the bright-
colored Game Tokens.

"Lights, please!" said the Owl pointing to the
ceiling. Instantly, the lights went out, and a solitary
spotlight shone down on Solomon.

The Owl stood silently for a while, as if gathering
up emotion for the coming performance. The cham-

ber was breathlessly still. Kris watched curiously. Suddenly, Solomon threw both wings up in the air and began:

I break windows with baseballs
And then Run Away!
I don't heed instruction,
I just Disobey.

I Lie and I Steal and I Pick
Rotten Friends!
I take Foooooooolish Turns that bring
Foooooooolish Ends.

Despite all my Folly,
I want to be Wise.
Now guess if you can
Whooooooo am I?

As Solomon finished this last stanza, he leaned forward and stared Kris in the eye. Kris bowed his head in shame.

"It's about me, huh?" he said, no longer feeling so proud.

"Kristopher my boy," said the Owl, placing a wing around Kris's shoulder, "you've done some very foolish things. . . . You can see that from the little Poem I've just recited. But I think you've learned your lesson . . . or a part of it anyway. You've started Thinking before Doing, and that's what this Wizzdom game is all about."

"I guess it started when I smashed the window

back at home, didn't it?" Kris admitted, staring down at his sneakers. "I am sorry, though. Really . . . I am."

"Sorry enough to go home to your parents?" said the Owl.

Kris nodded, then looked up at the Owl. Solomon stared at him for a long time. Then suddenly, he grabbed Kris's hand and held it high in the air shouting, "I hereby pronounce Kristopher Atwood, reigning champion of Hoomania!"

The crowd burst into their loudest applause yet, cheering and shouting and chanting Kris's name. But the Owl held up his wing once more and silenced the room.

"BUT!" he said abruptly, and he turned to face Kris. "You must remember that this Journey continues on at home! Every day, new adventures will rise to meet you. New Choices. New Shortcuts. New Tricks, and Slippery People of every sort!" The Owl looked him in the eye one last time (very seriously) and added, "With that in mind, Kristopher Atwood . . . I bid you farewell!"

Again, the assembly of Game People broke into applause. They crowded around Kris cheering him like a hero and hoisted him up into the air. Then with a mighty shout, they threw him up into the air amidst a shower of floating balloons and banners.

As he fell back toward the ground, they caught him up again and gathered their strength for one last throw. Together they counted: One. . . . Two. . . .

Three, and hurled Kris high into the air, cheering as he soared toward the crystal ceiling. But before he could fall back toward the ground, a sudden *FLASH* of blue light shot out of the crystal Gates and engulfed him.

10
A More Important Decision

The glowing pool of blue light sucked Kris through the air like an enormous vacuum. The world of Hoomania had disappeared and all that existed was spinning, falling, flickering swells of blue. As he tumbled through emptiness, Kris could feel himself growing at an incredible speed, and the next thing he knew, *THUD!* . . . He had landed on solid earth.

For a moment he was so shaken that he couldn't tell quite where he was. Then he realized that he was sitting on a grassy lawn. He had a baseball glove in one hand and a bat in the other.

"Weird," he thought.

But looking up, he soon found an explanation. Directly in front of him was his house. . . . And

94

there was the big picture window, smashed into teeny, little, jagged pieces! He got ready to jump to his feet, but hesitated. Inside the broken window, Kris could see his parents staring at the mess on the floor. Suddenly, Mrs. Atwood looked up and spotted him.

"There he is!" she shouted, poking her husband.

"Kristopher!" Mr. Atwood said, quite surprised.

"You stay right there, young man!" Mrs. Atwood added tersely. She grabbed her husband's arm and pulled him toward the door. Kris only had a few seconds before they'd be outside. What could he do? He wanted to jump up and run. He was sure he was in for a major scolding . . . probably twice as bad for running away. He couldn't tell them the story about Hoomania. . . . They'd never believe it in a million years! He could hear the door open, then slam sharply. He'd have to run for it now or never!

But Kris just couldn't budge. For some strange reason, it didn't seem like the right thing to do anymore. His decision was made. He sat patiently on the lawn waiting for whatever was going to happen to happen. He had no explanation, no excuse. "I'm doomed," he thought to himself. "Dead meat."

Mr. and Mrs. Atwood rushed out onto the front lawn and stared down at their son angrily. (Mr. Atwood was actually quite surprised that Kris hadn't run off and was still sitting there.) Mrs. Atwood held the baseball out in front of Kris's face and tried to say something. But she was so angry, she could only manage a few noises.

"I'm real sorry, Mom," Kris said desperately (and he looked it).

"How do you explain this? Playing baseball in front of the window, Kris! You know better," Mr. Atwood reprimanded.

"Yeah . . . I know," Kris agreed, hanging his head. "I didn't mean to. . . . I just. . . . Anyway . . . I'm sorry." He looked up apologetically. "I . . . I can probably do some jobs and get some money to buy a new one!"

"That's not the point, Son," his father began.

"You'll do a lot more than that, young man!" Mrs. Atwood finally exploded. "And you'll be grounded for a good long time . . . and. . . ." Suddenly both of Kris's parents looked at each other. This wasn't the typical punishment scene with their son. Usually Kris denied everything; he argued about detentions; he blamed other people; he pouted. But this time, Kristopher Atwood was admitting his mistake and offering to do something about it. Neither of his parents knew how to handle this sort of thing. . . . After all, he did say he was sorry.

There was a long silence where everyone looked at each other and felt rather confused. Finally, Mr. Atwood spoke up. "Well . . . something's going to be done anyway," he said in a very fatherly way. "We'll talk about it later . . . your mother and I. For now you can—"

"For now, you can go to your room," Mrs. Atwood completed the sentence. "And don't you come out until we call you for dinner!"

Kris got up and walked slowly towards the house. He felt a little sulky, but really, things hadn't gone all that badly. And as he started inside the door, he began to think about Hoomania.

It struck him: He had been *inside* Hoomania! Wow! He wondered if Mr. Weatherfield would let him play the game again sometime—even though he didn't plan on getting in anymore trouble real soon.

Mr. and Mrs. Atwood watched their son go into the house. He had gone obediently. He hadn't whined or argued or kicked things. Neither of them really wanted to punish him at all. In fact, they were both a little worried.

As Kris closed the door, he heard his mother say, "Do you think something's wrong, honey?"

"I don't know. It's . . . it's just not like Kris."

"Maybe he's going through some sort of stage," Mrs. Atwood suggested.

"Could be," her husband concurred. "Or . . . maybe he's just starting to grow up."

Kris spent the next three days indoors being grounded. He found some satisfaction in the fact that it rained for two of those days. But he also made excellent use of that time to write a diary of his journeys inside Hoomania. However, after two days of writing about adventures and drawing detailed illustrations, he was quite bored with being indoors and quite anxious to get back to the business of being a kid.

In fact, as soon as his grounding was over, he intended to hurry straight over to Mr. Weatherfield's workshop and find out if there were any other games he could play. He imagined that Mr. Weatherfield must have dozens of other fantastic things that Kris hadn't seen yet.

And just as he was thinking about this, a sudden *rap-a-rap-a-rap*! came at the window. Kris turned around in his desk chair and was quite surprised. For, outside his window, hovering in the air, was the oddest little flying machine that he'd ever seen. No bigger than a shoe box, the machine was shaped like a submarine and had three spinning propellers on top. A little extension arm had come out of its nose cone and was tapping on Kris's window.

It seemed to want Kris to open the window; so he did, and then got quickly out of the way. As soon as he had stepped aside, a tiny rocket flew out from under the machine and thundered into Kris's room. It circled overhead several times making an awful racket. Then a big cloud of smoke burst out of its tail pipes, a parachute popped open, and the little rocket floated to the bedroom floor. The flying machine outside the window honked its squeaky horn and flew away.

Kris approached the strange, little rocket with a great deal of caution. He reached down to touch it, and just as he did, it snapped in two and a small flag shot up into the air. Kris jumped back at first. But on a second look, he could see that the flag was actually some sort of note. He took it from the rocket and sat down to read it:

To: Kristopher Atwood, Runaway, Explorer, and Champion of Hoomania

From: Samuel T. Weatherfield, Inventor

Dearest Kristopher,

How do you like my new invention, the PS-2000 Aerial Correspondence Transport Device? I hope it didn't startle you, but I felt that I ought to send you a quick note after watching a little of your adventure through Hoomania.

I see that you've won the game and that you managed to patch things up at home. It appears that you've learned a lot from your short journey.

But I'm writing because I wanted to be sure that you understand what all this "wisdom" business is about. I believe I once told you that wisdom is making decisions that please God. Well, that sounds quite simple, but lots of times we get so excited about what *we* want, that we don't stop to think about what *He* has in mind. I think that's what happened the day you ran away.

You see, the world is a good deal like that game *Hoomania*. When you get off the proper path (that is, when you start looking for trouble), things go all wrong. Usually other people get hurt, and in the end, you're always worse off. Worse than that, it displeases God because it means you don't respect His wisdom. If you *do* trust His wisdom, then you'll think before you do things (as you have started doing quite well, I might add!)—mostly you'll think about how things might affect other people.

I plan to check up on you regularly. (I have several other games that will do just the trick!) So, why don't you drop by my shop as soon as you're out of "prison." I might be able to put you to work on a few of my latest inventions. I might even be able to keep you out of trouble!

Much love,
Sam

HOOMANIA—A JOURNEY THROUGH THE BOOK OF PROVERBS

is also available on 16 mm. film for rental by contacting your local Christian film library. Length: 37 minutes; $39.00.

HOOMANIA is also available on video for use in home and small group, face-to-face instructional settings. Length: 37 minutes; $29.95.

Contact Gospel Films, Inc., or your local Christian bookstore.

SATCH AND THE NEW KID

A new kid in town . . .

And he's the same age as Satch, Spinner, Pete, and A.J.—the Fearless Foursome. He'll fit right in—spitting cherry pits for distance, joining the secret club, and avoiding pests of little brothers. Best of all, he's a soccer star—just what the team needs to win this year's championship.

But something's wrong between the new kid and A.J., and Satch feels caught in the middle. He likes Hai—the new kid. But he likes A.J., too, and he's known A.J. forever. Can't he be friends with both of them? Why can't they get along?

It looks like trouble coming—fast!

***Read about Satch and the gang
in these exciting books!***

Satch and the New Kid
Satch and the Motormouth

KAREN SOMMER teaches third graders and has twin boys of her own. Her writing career began when her students begged for more of the stories she composed for class. She's been writing ever since!

SATCH AND THE MOTORMOUTH

Sixth grade's terrific!

Everyone likes Satch—including Miss Hepburn, the neatest teacher at Roosevelt School, who even makes spelling rules fun!

Satch only has one problem—Motormouth Marcie Cook. How can one girl be so loud and obnoxious? Of all the kids in class, why does *she* sit behind him? Why do they always end up having to work together—at church as well as at school? And he's pretty sure Marcie's responsible for the anonymous valentines he's getting.

Nothing could be worse! Or could it?

What about being covered with itchy chicken pox?

Or getting caught in a hailstorm of eggs?

Or a *silent* Marcie?

Read about Satch and the gang in these exciting books!

Satch and the New Kid
Satch and the Motormouth

KAREN SOMMER teaches third graders and has twin boys of her own. Her writing career began when her students begged for more of the stories she composed for class. She's been writing ever since!

MAKING CHOICES BOOKS

You're in Command!

MAKING CHOICES BOOKS let you create your own stories with the choices you make, page by page. It's great practice in Christian decision making. But, unlike real life, if you don't like the way things are turning out in your story, you can go back and start over! Over thirty possible endings.

A FAVORITE SERIES OF KIDS EVERYWHERE!

Ask for these Making Choices titles from Chariot Books

The Cereal Box Adventures
Flight into the Unknown
Dr. Zarnof's Evil Plot
Mr. X's Golden Scheme
The President's Stuck in the Mud and
Other Wild West Escapades
Trouble in Quartz Mountain Tunnel
A Horse Named Funny Bits
Help! I'm Drowning!
Help! I'm Shrinking!
Avalanche!
The Hawaiian Computer Mystery
Dog Food and Other Delights
General K's Victory Tour